Rose at
Rocky Ridge

THE ROSE
CHAPTER BOOK COLLECTION

Adapted from the Rose Years books
by Roger Lea MacBride
Illustrated by Doris Ettlinger

LITTLE HOUSE

Rose #2

Rose at Rocky Ridge

ADAPTED FROM THE ROSE YEARS BOOKS BY

Roger Lea MacBride

ILLUSTRATED BY

Doris Ettlinger

HarperTrophy®
A Division of HarperCollins*Publishers*

Adaptation by Heather Henson.

HarperCollins®, 📖®, Little House®, Harper Trophy®, and The Rose Years™
are trademarks of HarperCollins Publishers Inc.

Rose at Rocky Ridge
Text adapted from *Little House on Rocky Ridge*,
text copyright 1993 by Roger Lea MacBride.
Illustrations by Doris Ettlinger
Illustrations copyright © 2000 by Renée Graef
Copyright © 2000 by HarperCollins Publishers

Library of Congress Cataloging-in-Publication Data
MacBride, Roger Lea.
  Rose at Rocky Ridge : adapted from The Rose years books / by Roger
Lea MacBride ; illustrated by Doris Ettlinger.
    p.   cm. — (A Little house chapter book)
"Rose #2."
Summary: When Rose Wilder and her parents arrive in Missouri, they must
work hard to make a rundown farm into their own home.
  ISBN 0-06-028156-1 (lib. bdg.) — ISBN 0-06-442093-0 (pbk.)
  1. Lane, Rose Wilder, 1886–1968—Juvenile fiction. [1. Lane, Rose Wilder,
1886–1968—Fiction.   2. Frontier and pioneer life—Missouri—Fiction.
3. Farm life—Missouri—Fiction. 4. Missouri—Fiction.] I. Ettlinger, Doris,
ill.   II. Title.   III. Series.
PZ7.M12255Ro   2000   99-31386
[Fic]—DC21   CIP
                                  ❖
First Harper Trophy edition, 2000

Contents

CHAPTER 1

A New Home

Rose Wilder sat on the wagon seat between Mama and Papa. Her little dog Fido sat on Mama's lap. Rose was excited. They were on their way to their new home.

Rose had spent the whole summer traveling in the covered wagon. Mama and Papa had decided to leave the South Dakota prairie and move to a part of Missouri called The Land of the Big Red Apple.

The Cooleys had traveled with them.

Rose had played with her friends, Paul and George Cooley, when the wagons had stopped along the trail. Paul was the oldest, George was eight, and Rose was seven and a half. They were great friends.

But now summer was almost over and they were all living in Missouri. Papa had bought a little farm where they would grow apples. Rose couldn't wait to see it.

"Is it far?" Rose asked.

"Just on the other side of town," Mama answered.

Rose grinned happily. They weren't going far away at all.

Papa drove the wagon through town. They passed the hotel where the Cooleys were living. Mr. Cooley had said he'd had enough of farming. He wanted to run a hotel. Paul and George were town boys now. Rose was going to be a country girl.

Outside of town, they passed a tall, square building. It had big windows all around it and a bell tower on top.

"That's the schoolhouse where you'll go to school," Mama said.

"Will Paul and George go there, too?" Rose asked.

"Of course," said Mama. "It's the only school in town."

Rose let out a little sigh of relief. She watched everything with bright eyes as the road dipped into the woods. The wagon went through a leafy tunnel of trees.

Soon Papa turned the horses off the road. Rose could see a faint set of wagon tracks running out in front of them through a little valley. A sparkling stream rippled beside them as they drove.

After a while, Papa stopped the wagon beside the stream. The horses bent their heads down to drink the clear water.

"Here we are!" Mama sang out. "What do you think?"

Rose looked up at the green hills around them. She didn't see a farm, or anything that looked like apple trees.

Papa tightened the reins and whistled to the horses. They raised their heads and leaned forward to pull the wagon across the stream. The wagon rolled up a hill and came to a stop in a clearing.

A little log house sat on one side of the clearing under some tall trees. Dead branches and old leaves covered the roof. Sticks and half-cut logs were piled on the ground.

The little log house looked lonely and run-down. But Rose thought it was the

 4

most beautiful house in the world. She scrambled over Mama's lap and climbed down the wagon wheel. She ran right up to the open door and peered inside.

The first room was a lean-to. It was narrow with slanted walls and a slanted roof. There was a hole in the ceiling for a stove pipe. The earth floor was covered with dead leaves.

The next room was bigger. It had a wooden floor and it was very dark. The little house had no windows at all.

Inside, the big room smelled like the woods. Dead leaves had blown into the corners. The floor squeaked as Rose walked.

"Rose!" Mama called from outside. "Come and help unload. It'll be dark soon."

Rose ran back outside. She found Fido sniffing around a pile of brush. His ears and tail stood straight up.

Rose began to carry a chair into the little house, but Mama stopped her.

"We're going to spend one more night in the wagon," Mama said.

"Can't we sleep in the little house, Mama?" Rose asked.

"Not until we scrub it, top to bottom,"

Mama told her.

As the sun went down, Rose watched the tall trees around them. The woods turned a ghostly gray. Everything became quiet and still. It seemed to Rose like the trees were listening.

In the silence Rose heard the soft sound of water bubbling. The sound came from behind the house. She knew it must be a little creek. It seemed to Rose like the water was laughing.

Rose wanted to go find the creek, but there were so many dark shadows now. She felt a little afraid. She couldn't wait until daylight to explore their new little farm.

CHAPTER 2

Cleaning House

Early the next morning, Rose gathered wood for the breakfast fire. Then Mama asked her to fetch a pail of water. Now Rose could find that laughing water.

She followed a little path. It went right from the door of the log house down a steep hill. At the bottom of the hill was a spring. The spring ran from behind a big rock into a little pool. The pool was clear and round.

Rose dipped a hand into the pool. The water was icy cold. It made her skin tingle.

After breakfast, Papa went off to cut trees. He had hired a man named Cyrus to help him. Papa and Cyrus would cut the trees into logs. Then Papa would sell the logs in town.

Rose helped Mama wash the breakfast dishes and put them away. Then they looked all around the little house. Inside, sunlight shone through the open door and peeked through the cracks in the wall.

"We'll have to get Papa to fill in those cracks," Mama said. "And then put in a window. This is the darkest place I ever saw."

Just then they heard a gunshot in the distance.

"Maybe Papa found us a rabbit for supper," said Mama.

Rose helped Mama scoop out the old ashes from the fireplace. They knocked down all the spiderwebs. Mama used the broom and Rose used a stick. Spiders scurried across the floor and walls. Rose's arms and legs crawled with imaginary spiders. She kept rubbing her skin to get rid of the tingly feeling.

Then they swept all the dust and the balls of spider thread and the mouse nests and the dead leaves out the door.

Next, Mama went to the creek and filled a pail with clean sand. She sprinkled the sand on the wood floor, along with some water. Together Mama and Rose got down on their hands and knees and scrubbed the floor with wet rags. They scrubbed as hard as they could.

Scrubbing the floor was the hardest work Rose had ever done. After a while, her arm ached and her back hurt. Her knuckles burned from scraping them

 10

against the floorboards. Her knees were sore from grinding into the grit. Sand got between her toes and under her finger-nails. It even got on her face.

But finally the sand had scrubbed all the dark, dirty wood. Rose and Mama rinsed it with buckets and buckets of fresh water from the spring.

On every trip to the spring, Rose and Mama stopped to drink some of the delicious water. Rose couldn't get enough of it. Her stomach sloshed and gurgled when she moved.

After the floor was clean, Mama said they could rest awhile. They sat on a log and watched Papa and Cyrus cut a tall tree with the big two-handed saw.

Papa pulled one end of the saw and Cyrus pushed. Then Cyrus pulled and Papa pushed. When they had cut almost

11

all the way through, the tree gave out a loud groan. Then it went crashing down, sending up a cloud of leaves and dust.

As they rested, Mama and Rose talked about how they should arrange the furniture in the little house.

"Where shall we put the big bed?" Mama asked.

Rose thought for a minute. "By the fireplace," she said. "To stay warm in winter."

"That's a good idea," Mama said.

Rose was thinking about where to put the other furniture, when suddenly Mama screamed and jumped up off the log. She grabbed her skirt in both hands and shook it hard.

"Rose," she shouted. "Come away from that log!"

Rose was so surprised she couldn't move. She looked where Mama had been

 12

sitting. At first she couldn't believe her eyes.

Staring back at her from the log was the biggest spider she had ever seen. It was as big as Papa's hand! Its long thick legs were covered in black fur.

The spider reached out with its front legs and began to crawl straight toward Rose!

Rose leaped up. She could hardly

breathe. She picked up a stick and stood there. She was ready to hit the spider, but she was afraid to try. The spider was so big it might chase her!

"I've never seen a spider so big!" Mama said.

They watched as the spider reached out with its giant legs. It was scary and beautiful at the same time. Rose couldn't take her eyes off it.

Papa and Cyrus came running. Papa had his rifle and Cyrus carried the ax.

"What is it, Bess?" Papa cried.

"Just look," Mama said, pointing.

They all looked. But the log was bare. The spider was gone.

"It was a spider," Mama said. "As big as my hand and covered with hair!"

Papa twisted his mustache. His eyes twinkled.

 14

Cyrus leaned on the ax and let out a chuckle. Mama glared at him.

"Sorry, ma'am," he said. "I didn't mean no offense. I guess them critters would give anybody a good fright that never seen one."

"What is it?" asked Rose.

"It's a tarantula," Cyrus said. "Don't worry, ma'am—they're not poisonous."

"I have never had such a fright," said Mama, laughing at herself. Then she turned to Papa. "I heard your gun, Manly. Did you get a rabbit for supper?"

"Rattlesnake," said Papa. "We killed one this morning."

"Rattlesnakes and huge hairy spiders," said Mama with a shudder. "What else will we find in these woods?"

Rose's eyes went wide. She looked all around her. She wondered if she would like living in Missouri after all.

15

CHAPTER 3

Moving In

All afternoon Rose thought about the big, black, hairy spider. She was jumpy during dinner. She was jumpy as she helped Mama unpack the wagon. She looked before she sat down. She kicked at piles of leaves.

Mama was thinking about the spider, too. She looked into boxes before she reached her hand inside. She scratched her ankles as if something were crawling on them. Seeing Mama scratch made Rose itch, too.

 16

After dinner, Rose helped Mama take the big bed out of the wagon. Then they brought out Rose's little trundle bed. They set the beds in the corner of the house, near the fireplace, right where Rose had suggested. The little trundle bed fit right under the big bed.

Mama brought the table inside and put it on the other side of the fireplace, near the door.

Together they cleaned out the little camp stove and put it in the lean-to. Mama would never have to cook outdoors again.

The trunks were too heavy to lift without Papa's help. So they opened the trunks in the wagon and carried the things in a little at a time.

First they brought in the linen and the clothing. Mama put the hanging clothes

17

on a rope tied between two rafters.

Rose helped Mama make up the big bed. Mama shook the crisp sheets open with a sharp *snap*! The musty smell of the trunk was in those sheets. For a moment Rose thought about her old home on the prairie.

After they were finished with the big bed, Rose made up the trundle bed by herself. She tucked the corners of the sheets in snugly, just the way Mama made the big bed. Then she laid her quilt on top and smoothed it out.

Now her bed was all tidy. It was ready to crawl into. They were going to sleep inside their new home that night!

After the beds were made, Rose carefully helped carry in Mama's beautiful china plates. Rose was happy to see those plates again. She was tired of the flimsy tin plates they used for camping.

In the bottom of one trunk, Mama found the rag rug Aunt Carrie had braided for a going-away present. She spread it in front of the fireplace. It gave the little house a cheerful look.

Then she brought in the wooden clock and set it on the mantel.

"Now, let's put out the green table-cloth, and we're finished," Mama said.

After the tablecloth was all smoothed out, Mama stood back in the doorway. She put her hands on her hips and looked at the room.

Just then the clock chimed five times. Every corner of the house filled with the clear, round sound. The little house seemed to be brimming with life.

"Time to think about supper," Mama said.

19

When it was dark, Papa came home from cutting wood. Mama and Rose went outside and helped him stack the stove wood. Then they washed their hands and faces in the basin Mama had set on a chair just outside the door.

Papa started to walk into the little house, but Mama stopped him.

"Shoes off, if you please," she said with a smile.

Papa pulled off his shoes and sighed with relief. "Ahh," he said, rubbing his ankles.

"Wait just one minute," Mama said. She disappeared behind the door into the house. Rose heard the clink of the lamp chimney being lifted, and the sound of a match striking.

Rose quickly wiped her bare feet on the doorsill. Then she scurried through the door into the house. She wanted to see Papa's face when he came in.

"You may come in now," Mama called to Papa.

Papa opened the door slowly. His tired eyes shone happily in the dim light.

"Well, I'll be . . ." he said, slowly looking around the room.

Rose looked, too. So did Mama.

The glow from the lamp made everything seem so cozy.

Mama had already put the food on the table. The bread platter sat in the middle with three big pieces of crusty corn bread on it. The air was rich with the creamy smell of beans bubbling on the stove.

The little sewing chest Papa had made for Mama gleamed in the lamplight. The quilt that family and friends had made for them before they left the prairie lay on the

21

big bed. Papa's good hat hung from a peg by the front door.

Papa went over and picked up his hat.

"A fellow knows he's home when he has a place to hang his hat," said Papa.

Mama looked at him with soft eyes. Her face glowed with pride.

Papa gave Mama a great hug and kiss. Then he picked Rose up by the waist and held her high over his head. He gave her a big, bristly kiss, too, and hugged her hard.

"And now," Papa said. "I'm sure we could all do with some supper. I'm as hungry as a grizzly bear."

CHAPTER 4

Rocky Ridge

One morning a few days later, Rose watched Papa load the wagon with the rest of the wood. Papa clicked his tongue at the horses, and the wagon began to rumble down the hill.

"Good luck," Mama called after Papa.

"Don't wait for me for supper," Papa called back, waving his hat. "I won't be home until the whole wagonload is sold!"

Rose listened until the wagon's rumble died away. She knew Papa was driving over the far hill, into Mansfield. She wondered if he would see her friends George and Paul Cooley. She hoped Papa would be able to sell all the wood.

After Papa left, Mama and Rose did their morning chores. They washed the breakfast dishes. They made the beds and swept out the house.

When they were finished, Mama said, "Let's go soak our feet in the spring."

Rose and Mama followed the little path down to the spring. They sat on rocks at the edge of the water. The sunshine was warm. It made wavy lines at the bottom of the pool.

Slowly, Rose lowered her feet and legs into the cold, clear water. Her skin tingled. She broke out in shivery goosebumps.

Mama took off her shoes. She sighed as she dipped her toes into the water.

"This is nice," Mama said.

25

"Where are the apple trees, Mama?"
Rose asked.

"Just over the hill," Mama answered.
"We'll walk there later."

"Will we be able to eat the apples
soon?" Rose asked.

"No," said Mama. "The apple trees
are young. They won't grow apples for
another five or six years."

Rose was shocked. She counted on her

fingers. She would be thirteen by the time she could eat her own apples!

After sitting for a while, they climbed the steep hill above the spring. The hill was thick with trees. The ground was rocky.

"I'm sorry I left my shoes by the pool," Mama said. She stepped carefully over a rocky spot. "These sharp stones hurt my feet."

Rose's feet were tough from going barefoot all summer. She didn't even notice those rocks.

When they came to the top of the hill, they were almost high enough to see across the whole valley, all the way to town. They could see the bell tower of the school poking up above the trees.

Rose and Mama walked down the other side of the hill and into a big clearing. There were rows and rows of little trees

27

laid out on their sides. There were more trees than Rose could count.

"Those are the apple trees," Mama said. "They are waiting to be planted in the orchard."

Rose looked at the trees in surprise. They were much smaller than any of the apple trees she had seen as they drove through Missouri.

Rose and Mama walked a little farther. They came to a field where some of the trees had already been planted. The trees were very far apart. They stuck up from small mounds of dirt. There were stumps here and there. And there were brush piles along the edge of the field.

Rose felt a little disappointed. Their orchard didn't look anything like the beautiful, tidy orchards they had passed.

"The trees are so small," Rose said.

"Will they ever get big enough to make apples?"

"Before you know it, the branches of those little trees will grow until one day they can touch one another," Mama answered. "And then folks in Kansas City and Memphis will be baking our apples into their pies."

Rose looked at those tiny, fragile trees. She could hardly believe it. She thought about being thirteen and picking their first apples. She couldn't imagine being that old.

Mama and Rose walked around the rest of the farm. The land was all woods. Mama said that Papa and Cyrus would have to cut a lot of trees that winter to get the orchard planted in time for spring.

The ground was rocky almost everywhere. In some places, huge boulders stuck up from the dirt. But Mama said that

29

someday they would have smooth, rolling meadows.

"For now, it is a very rocky ridge of land," said Mama. She looked at Rose and her face suddenly lit up. "We can call the farm Rocky Ridge. What do you think?"

Rose liked the sound of it. It was easy to say, and it was true. The farm was full of rocks.

"I like it," she said.

"That's it, then," Mama said happily. "We'll tell Papa tonight."

Rose smiled. She couldn't wait until Papa came home from town.

 30

CHAPTER 5

Building a Henhouse

Every morning, Rose helped Mama water and feed the chickens. During the day, the hens ran free. Fido kept them safe from hawks and other creatures. He even helped Mama and Rose find the hens' nests. And he didn't eat a single egg.

Each afternoon, Rose and Mama collected all the eggs they could find. Then Rose went where Papa and Cyrus were chopping wood to get clean sawdust. She held her skirt out like a sack. Papa helped her scoop the sawdust up into her skirt.

Inside the lean-to, Rose helped Mama sprinkle the sawdust into an old feed-sack. Then Mama laid in some eggs and sprinkled more sawdust on top. She kept making layers of sawdust and eggs until she was out of eggs. Then she threw the leftover sawdust on the earth floor to keep the mud down.

When Papa went to town, he took the sack to the store and traded the eggs for things they needed, like flour and salt pork. Sometimes Papa brought home a treat for Rose, like a new hair ribbon or a piece of stick candy.

At sundown each day, the chickens flew into the branches of a big tree to sleep. Fido could not protect them there.

 32

One night, Rose woke up to a horrible screeching. Fido was barking loudly.

"What is it?" Rose cried.

Mama hurried to light the lantern. Then she bolted for the door.

"Wait," Papa shouted. He snatched his rifle off the wall and hurried to catch up with Mama.

The horrible screeching stopped. Rose sat up in bed. She wondered what could have made such a terrible noise.

"An owl carried off one of the chickens," Mama told Rose when she and Papa came back inside.

In the morning, Rose found white chicken feathers scattered on the ground near the tree.

That day, Cyrus helped Papa build a henhouse to keep the chickens safe at night. The henhouse would be square with a slanted roof so the rain would roll right off.

Papa and Cyrus started by laying small tree trunks, one on top of another. They notched the ends, so all the trunks fit together snugly. Then Papa and Cyrus sealed the cracks with clay mud from the creek. They made sure there were no spaces for the cold air to blow in, or for snakes to sneak through.

Papa built a door big enough for Mama and Rose to go in and out. Then Papa built a little door for the chickens. There was a wooden latch to keep the doors closed. Mama showed Rose how to use it.

"The doors must always be closed at night, after the chickens are in," Mama told Rose. "Otherwise, a raccoon or a fox could walk right in."

Finally, Papa made a ladder and two

wooden shelves for the chickens to nest on.

"We need lots of leaves to put on the floor," Mama told Rose. "Chickens like to have dry feet."

Rose went to the woods and gathered leaves. She carried them to the henhouse in her skirt. She made many trips with her skirt full of leaves. Finally the floor was covered.

But when sundown came, none of the chickens would go near the henhouse. They just stretched their necks and looked up at their old tree.

"Let's try herding them," said Mama. "But gently. If we scare them, they won't lay eggs."

Mama stood on one side of the chickens, and Rose stood on the other. Slowly, they walked toward the henhouse, trying to shoo the chickens toward the door. But when they got close to the henhouse, the chickens darted past Rose and Mama into the clearing.

Next Mama made a little trail of cornmeal on the ground, leading to the henhouse door. She scattered a handful inside. The chickens greedily pecked up all the cornmeal on the ground. When they got to the door, they cocked their heads and looked at it. But then they scooted away.

Mama and Rose couldn't help laughing at the chickens.

Then Mama had another idea. She picked up two long straight branches for herself. She found two long straight branches for Rose. They held the sticks out at their sides, dragging on the ground. Now, it was harder for the chickens to sneak by them.

Mama and Rose herded the chickens

 36

into a little crowd. The nervous chickens walked around in circles, cackling, squawking, and flapping their wings. They milled noisily in front of the henhouse's little door.

But still they refused to go in.

"Well, that does it," Mama said, throwing away the sticks. "If we get them too riled up, they won't lay eggs for weeks. Maybe they need a day or so to get used

to the henhouse."

In a few minutes, all the chickens had flown up into the tree.

The next day, Mama left the henhouse doors open. She spread more cornmeal on the floor of the henhouse and set the water bowl nearby.

The chickens went into the henhouse and ate all the cornmeal. They drank the water. But when sundown came, they marched out of the henhouse and flew up into the tree.

Every night, Mama and Rose tried to herd the chickens using the sticks. One night, a few chickens went into the henhouse through the big door. So Mama locked them in for the night.

The next night, a few more chickens went in. The rest flew up into the tree.

Finally, one evening, all the chickens

let Mama and Rose herd them into the henhouse.

Then for a long time after that, the chickens did a funny thing. When anyone picked up a long stick, or carried a broom, the chickens ran into the henhouse.

CHAPTER 6

Making a Window

Fall came and went on Rocky Ridge Farm. The leaves on the trees turned bright red and sunshine yellow. The acorns began to fall from the oak tree next to the little house. When the wind blew, the acorns tapped and rattled over the wooden roof. It sounded to Rose like little animals were running around above her head.

Soon, the leaves began to fall from the trees like soft, crinkly rain. Rose liked to walk through the crunchy piles.

40

The crisp air was full of butterflies. There were small bright-yellow ones and black and orange ones.

One morning, Rose stepped outside to gather wood for the stove. The forest was hidden behind a curtain of thick, cottony fog. She had never seen anything so strange. She could hear Papa's voice talking to the horses. She could hear the chickens clucking. But she could not see anything through the fog.

After breakfast, the sun began to burn through the fog. Then Rose noticed something else. During the night, spiders had spun webs everywhere. There were spiderwebs draped across the grass like tiny lace tablecloths. There were spiderwebs at the edges of the roof. Spiderwebs clung to the wagon spokes.

Each silky thread was dotted with tiny

water beads. The water had been left by the fog. When the sun shone through, the webs sparkled like diamond necklaces.

Later in the morning, Rose noticed that the sun had dried out all the webs. By dinnertime, Rose could not find any webs or any spiders. But the next morning, the webs were there all over again.

Mornings were chilly now. When Rose got out of bed, the air felt as cool as the water in the spring.

"Time to fill in the cracks in the cabin walls," Papa said, shivering as he pulled on his shoes.

Right after breakfast, he went to the creek and brought back a bucket of reddish-brown clay. All around the outside of the house he stuffed and hammered chips of wood into the spaces between the logs. Then he smeared clay around the chips, to seal up the holes.

"Can I help, Papa?" Rose asked.

"Of course you can," said Papa. "You plug the holes down at the bottom. I'll do the ones up high."

Together they smeared clay into all those holes and cracks between the logs. Rose liked the smooth feel of the clay. She tried hard to do a tidy job.

When Papa looked down to see how

she was doing, he let out a great hearty laugh.

"Why, you're as dirty as a mud fence after a rain," he said. He brushed a bit of dried clay from her cheek. "But look what a fine job you're doing. Nothing can get through those cracks now."

When they were done, the little log house was warm and cozy. But it was very dark, especially with the door closed.

So Papa told Mama he would make her a window. He got his ax, hammer, and chisel.

Mama was excited. She pointed to a place on the wall where she wanted the window.

"That way I can see the sunset when I'm inside making supper," she said.

"Very well, Bess," said Papa.

First, Papa cut a square into the logs.

The square was about two logs high. Then he made a frame from smooth boards. He made holes in the boards and in the logs. He took his knife and carved eight wooden pegs. Then he hammered the wooden pegs through the boards and the logs. The frame was good and snug.

Papa measured the window frame carefully. Then he rode into town. He came back with a piece of glass in a wooden frame. He carefully set that frame inside the frame he had made. Now they had a real window that opened and closed.

Finally, Papa made a leather catch so the window could be shut tight.

Mama and Papa and Rose stood back to admire it.

"It's just beautiful!" said Mama. "The house seems bigger and friendlier."

Rose looked out the window through

the trees. So many leaves had fallen. She could now see all the way to the little valley. Rose knew that winter was on the way.

CHAPTER 7

Rabbit Stew

Each day was full of chores on Rocky Ridge Farm. Mama and Papa had their own chores to do. And so did Rose.

First thing in the morning, Rose made sure there was enough wood by the stove. Then she peeled potatoes, or sorted beans, or stirred cornmeal. She set the table before meals. And she helped wash and dry the dishes after. Then she put them away in the dish box.

After breakfast, she swept the cabin and made her little trundle bed. Then she pushed it under the big bed.

She carried buckets of water for the chickens, for the horses, for cooking, for laundry, for the washbasin, for the dishes, for housecleaning, for Saturday baths, and for drinking.

She fed the chickens and gathered eggs. Once a week, she helped Mama clean the old leaves out of the henhouse. Then they put down a bed of fresh leaves.

Some days there were special chores to do on top of the regular ones.

On Mondays, Rose helped Mama wash the clothes. She stirred the big tin basin full of steaming-hot water. She wasn't strong enough to scrub their dresses and Papa's overalls. But she could scrub the socks. Then she helped Mama rinse everything three times. When they were done rinsing, they hung it all up to dry.

On Tuesdays, Rose helped Mama with ironing.

On Fridays, they cleaned the whole house, from the rafters to the floors.

On Saturdays, Mama baked bread. Rose helped her mix the dough.

In between all of the chores, there was mending and sewing to do. And Rose had her lessons.

With so many chores every day, there was hardly any time for playing, except on Sundays.

On Sundays, Mama and Papa and Rose still got up early to do their morning chores. The horses had to be fed and watered, no matter what day it was. The chickens and the eggs had to be taken care of. Wood had to be gathered.

But after breakfast, Mama read to them from the Bible. Then Papa took a nap and Mama wrote in her journal, or she wrote letters to Grandma and Grandpa. Rose sat by the fire and read one of Mama's books.

On Sundays, the air was always rich with the smell of dinner cooking on the stove. The little log house felt snug and cozy.

After dinner, Rose usually went outside to play fetch with Fido. Sometimes she felt a little lonely. She missed Paul and George Cooley.

Rose had made one friend since she moved to Rocky Ridge Farm. Her friend's name was Alva, and she lived with her family just over the hill. Alva had bright-red hair. She was different from any girl Rose had ever met. She wore overalls and she hunted and fished with her father. She told scary stories and was very smart. But

 50

Rose didn't always see Alva on Sundays.

Sometimes Rose poked around in the woods with Fido and looked for Indian arrowheads by the creek.

One Sunday she decided to try to climb the brushpile. The brushpile was where Papa put all the leftover branches he cut each day. It stood as high as the wagon.

Rose circled the brushpile. Then she tried stepping up onto it. The pile leaned to one side. It was hard to find a solid place to stand. Branches snapped under her feet. Every time she moved, her legs went plunging into the tangle of brush.

Finally, she made it to the very top. She was high above the ground.

The brushpile was very springy. Rose bounced up and down, a little at first. The branches bounced under her. Sticks and limbs crackled.

Rose bounced higher and higher, until the whole pile was bouncing.

Suddenly a rabbit darted out one side of the pile and bounded away into the bushes.

"Fido!" Rose shouted. But Fido was nowhere to be seen.

Rose clambered down as fast as she could and ran after the rabbit. She picked up a stick to beat the bushes away as she ran. The rabbit leaped out and went up the hill. Rose chased the rabbit up and down the hill. The rabbit ran through bushes and over rocks.

Soon Rose was out of breath. Her feet hurt from stubbing them on the rocks. She wondered if the rabbit was as tired as she was.

Just then Fido came running and

barking. He chased the rabbit right into a hollow log.

Rose got down on her hands and knees to look. She could see the shadow of the rabbit's head and ears. Fido whined and wagged his tail back and forth. He wanted to get into the log, but it was too small in the middle.

Rose found a big rock nearby. She pushed and rolled the rock over to the log. She pushed it into one end. Then she found another rock and pushed and rolled it against the other end.

Rose had caught a rabbit! She had done it all by herself. She knew Papa would be proud of her. She raced back to the log house to fetch him.

That night for supper there was fresh corn bread and rabbit stew. Fido got his share, too.

"My little prairie Rose is becoming quite the woodsman," said Papa at the table.

"Yes, Rose," Mama agreed. "What a nice plump rabbit."

But Rose did not feel like a woodsman. She had wanted to make Papa and Mama proud, but now she just looked at her plate. She was hungry, but she couldn't take one bite of that rabbit stew. She could only nibble a little of the corn bread.

"You've hardly touched your supper," Mama said. "Are you ill?"

"No," Rose said quietly. "I'm not very hungry."

Papa looked at Rose thoughtfully. He laid down his fork and wiped his mustache on his napkin.

"Come here," he said gently.

Rose went and sat on Papa's knee.

55

"You know," Papa said. "It was lucky you caught that rabbit for us."

"It was?" asked Rose.

"Yes, indeed," Papa answered. "We must all keep up our strength, to work this farm and build it. The rabbit you caught is helping us do that. So long as we can live off our land, we'll never go hungry."

"You can be proud," Mama said. "You helped feed this family."

Rose thought about that. She started to feel better.

She went back to her chair and looked at her plate. And then she remembered how much she liked Mama's stew.

CHAPTER 8

Barn Raising

One morning after Papa had left to do his chores, Mama told Rose they were going to clean the house from top to bottom.

"It isn't Friday yet," Rose said.

"Company's coming," said Mama. "The Cooleys and Alva's family."

Rose was surprised. "Paul and George? And Alva?" she asked. "Everyone's coming here?"

"Yes," said Mama. "They are coming to help us build our barn, and I want the

57

place to shine."

Mama took the broom and knocked the spiderwebs out of the rafters. Rose helped her dust the whole house. They hung the rag rug outside. Rose beat the dirt out of the rug with a stick.

Rose and Mama took the beds apart and fluffed up the mattresses. Mama hung the quilts and sheets outside in the fresh air. Then they scrubbed the floor with sand and rinsed it with spring water.

After the dinner dishes were put away, Rose helped with the cooking. Mama baked extra corn bread and rolled out pie crusts. Rose peeled enough apples for two pies. She was careful to keep the peels thin so nothing would go to waste.

All day long Rose thought about the things she would show Paul and George. And she couldn't wait to hear how they

 58

liked living in a hotel.

Just before supper, Mama put their best quilt on the bed. She laid out her second-best calico dress and Rose's blue school dress.

After supper, they all took baths and then they climbed into bed.

Early the next morning, they ate a cold breakfast so Mama could make a chicken pie.

Rose helped roll out the pie crust. Mama browned pieces of chicken in salt pork and laid them in the skillet. Then she sprinkled bits of salt pork and hard-boiled egg on the chicken and poured gravy over it all. Finally, she put the top crust on the pie and set the skillet in the fireplace. The pie would be ready by dinnertime.

Rose swept out the cabin again, and

then everything was ready.

The sun was just coming up when Fido barked. Rose could see the Cooleys' wagon driving up the hill. Right behind them came a second wagon. Rose saw Alva sitting on the seat between her mother and father.

"Say, Rose!" Paul shouted when the wagons came to a stop.

Everyone talked all at once. Rose was bursting with excitement. But she barely had time to say hello. There was another wagon coming up the hill, and another, and another.

Mama stared at the wagons. Papa let out a low whistle.

"Well, I'll be," he said.

The wagons pulled right up into the clearing. Men and women and children began pouring out of them.

"Who are all these strangers?" Mama asked Papa, her eyes wide.

"I'd say they've come to help," Papa answered.

Mama shook her head in disbelief. "How will I ever feed them all?" she asked.

"They brought food, Mama," Rose said. "Look."

The women on the wagon seats were handing down baskets with white cloths over them. Children were carrying pitchers and bowls. They were bringing all that food to the house.

Now the clearing was full of laughing voices. Women came to introduce themselves to Mama. They wore large bonnets and they had friendly smiles.

"Howdy, Mrs. Wilder. I'm Mrs. Lockwood," said one woman. "I brought some of my pickles today. I'll just set them over there."

"I'm Lydia Bates," said another woman.

Mama smiled shyly and thanked everyone. Mrs. Cooley helped Mama decide where to set all the food.

Papa spoke with the men about the barn raising. Their breath made a mist in the cold morning air.

Rose wanted to watch the barn being built and to play with her friends. But there was no time for that.

All morning, Rose and Alva ran in and out of the house helping the women prepare dinner. The little log house was crammed full of people. Rose hardly saw Paul and George. They were with the other boys, helping with the barn.

Rose and Alva took turns stirring the

iron pot of beans. The pot simmered over a pit fire outside. There were potatoes roasting in the ashes.

The neighbors had brought sweet potatoes and salt pork and smoked ham. There was fried chicken, and there were bowls of pickles and of sweet-and-tart corn relish. There were apple pies and persimmon puddings and doughnuts and gingerbread. And there were big pitchers of milk and apple cider.

All morning Rose heard the sound of logs crashing and axes ringing. She could hear the men groan and shout as they lifted the logs into place.

Finally, one of the women took a spoon and beat the bottom of an empty pail as loud as she could. The men let out a great cheer. Everyone was glad it was dinner-time.

The women had made long tables by laying planks across tree stumps. The planks were covered with pans and platters, bowls and pitchers, forks, spoons, plates, and cups.

Now that it was dinnertime, Rose could talk to her friends. She introduced Alva to Paul and George.

"Where do you live?" Alva asked. "I never seen you around here before."

"We live in town," Paul said. "In the Mansfield Hotel. My pa and ma run it."

"Well, that's something," said Alva. "I never been inside a hotel. What's it like?"

"It's the best place I ever lived," Paul replied.

Rose was surprised to see how much taller and older Paul looked.

"Pa sends me to meet the trains and the stagecoaches," Paul said. "Look, Rose.

Pa even gave me my own pocket watch."

Paul pulled a silver watch from his pants pocket and opened it. It was handsome and grown-up. It had a picture of a train engraved on the back.

"I greet the guests and carry their bags," Paul said, snapping the watch shut. "Sometimes they even give me a nickel tip!"

"Why?" asked Rose.

"For being helpful and polite, of course," Paul answered.

After dinner, the men went back to work. Rose and Alva helped wash the dishes. All the leftover food was packed away.

The women took out their knitting and sewing. They sat outside the house on logs and stumps, talking and laughing.

Mama told Rose she and Alva could go watch the men work on the barn.

The barn walls were already finished. Wood chips covered the ground like golden snowflakes. Now the men were working on the roof, so Paul and George could watch, too.

"Come on," Rose said. "I'll show you the apple trees."

On the way to the orchard, Rose told them about the tarantula. She told them how she and Fido had caught a rabbit.

"It sounds like fun living on a farm," George said. "We hardly ever get to play. You play all the time."

Rose knew better, but she didn't say a word.

"It's nice here, all right," Paul said. "But I still like town better."

Finally, when it was nearly time to start the evening chores, the last shingle was nailed into place. The barn was finished!

The women put their baskets back in the wagons. The men hitched their teams. Rose was sorry to see everyone go.

Mama and Papa went around and shook everyone's hand. Mama's face glowed. Rose waved to Paul and George and Alva until she couldn't see them anymore.

After the last wagon had rolled away, the woods seemed very still.

"Let's take a look, shall we?" said Papa.

The barn was much bigger than Rose had expected. Inside, there were two log rooms. In between the rooms was an open hallway. That was where Papa would put the wagon to keep it dry.

Rose ran into the open hallway and saw four large openings in one of the log rooms. Papa had made four stalls, one for each of the four horses. From now on, the horses would be safe and dry.

Rose helped Papa spread straw and dry leaves on the earthen floor of the new stalls. Then Papa led the horses in for the first time. The horses trotted with their heads held high.

After they were in their stalls, Papa visited each horse. He talked softly to them and stroked their necks, to make them feel at home.

When Mama, Papa, and Rose finally left the barn, the horses watched them go, looking at them through the openings in the logs.

Rose looked around the quiet clearing. They had made the lonely log cabin into a cozy home. Now they had a nice, safe house for the chickens, and a dry, sturdy barn for the horses. Soon, they might have cows, and maybe a few sheep. And one day, there would be apples on the apple trees. Rose was so proud of their little Rocky Ridge Farm.

Come Home to Little House!

THE CAROLINE
CHAPTER BOOK COLLECTION

Adapted from the Caroline Years books
by Maria D. Wilkes
Illustrated by Doris Ettlinger

THE COMPLETE
LAURA CHAPTER BOOK COLLECTION

Adapted from the Little House books
by Laura Ingalls Wilder
Illustrated by Renée Graef and Doris Ettlinger